Summer Visitors

Carol Barton

For Mark, Neil and Christian

Scholastic Children's Books
Commonwealth House, 1–19 New Oxford Street,
London WC1A 1NU, UK
a division of Scholastic Ltd
London ~ New York ~ Toronto ~ Sydney ~ Auckland

First published by Scholastic Ltd, 1997

ISBN 0 590 19250 7

Typeset by TW Typesetting, Midsomer Norton, Avon
Printed by Cox & Wyman Ltd, Reading, Berks.

10 9 8 7 6 5 4 3 2 1

Chapter 1

"But I didn't want to come here in the first place." Emma faced her mother across the small twin-bedded room they shared.

"I know you didn't, and I'm sorry, but really Emma, we don't have very much choice at the moment."

"I don't know anyone here," said Emma. "What am I going to do during the holidays?"

"Grandma says there is a family coming down from London to stay soon. Maybe you'll make friends with them. Please Emma, don't make a fuss," said Mum. "I haven't the time... I have to go and help Grandma in the dining-room."

"Can I go to the beach?" Emma asked as her mother reached the door.

Mum paused, one hand on the door handle, and looked back. "Yes, I suppose you can," she said. "But be careful, won't you?"

"Careful of what?" asked Emma. "You usually say be careful of the traffic – but there can't be any traffic on the beach."

"I know," said Mum, a bit impatiently Emma thought, "but there are other things … the sea, the rocks and cliffs. Grandma says they can all be very dangerous. Oh, and don't speak to strangers of course, but that applies wherever you are."

"I thought it was supposed to be a private beach," muttered Emma.

"It is," said Mum, "but you never know." With one, final, warning look she was gone.

Emma sat on the end of her bed and stared at the closed door then with a sigh she stood up and, crossing to the chest beneath the window, she opened the top drawer and pulled out a pair of pink lycra shorts and a white T-shirt.

Moments later, after she had changed out of

her jeans, Emma made her way down the two flights of stairs from the tiny attic room, past the many guest bedrooms and down to the ground floor of the hotel. Most of the guests had gone out but Emma could hear the clatter of dishes from the kitchen and the sound of the vacuum cleaner in the television lounge.

In the dining-room she caught sight of her mother as she set the tables for evening dinner, and through the open door of the tiny office Emma could hear her grandmother talking on the telephone.

Emma crept past both rooms. She knew if they caught sight of her they would start suggesting things she could do, and without even hearing them Emma knew she wouldn't want to do them.

The only thing she really wanted to do, she thought as she slipped out of the front door and into the hotel grounds, was to go home. To go back to the house in Mitchell Avenue, back to her best friend, Lucy, who lived next door, her other friends at school, and that rather nice new boy Simon Jefferies who had smiled at her on the last day of term.

At the time Emma had thought she would be going back to school after the summer holidays. At the time she hadn't known they were coming to live with her grandmother at Seahorse Bay.

Now it was all ruined. She frowned as she crossed the lawn still wet with dew. Now she wouldn't see Simon Jefferies ever again, she might never see Lucy again. Her stomach gave a sudden lurch at the possibility. Mum had said Lucy could come and see her when the season was over, but by then Lucy might have made new friends, while she, Emma would have no one. Mum had said she would make friends, but Emma didn't see how she could when there didn't seem to be anyone around of her own age.

"Morning, Miss."

Emma looked up sharply. She'd become so lost in her miserable thoughts that the voice made her jump. Samuel Moses, her grandmother's gardener and general handyman, was weeding one of the flower beds. "Oh, hello, Samuel," she said.

"Going to the beach?" Samuel carefully

straightened up, pushing his cap to the back of his head. He had worked at the Seahorse Bay Hotel longer than anyone could remember, even before Emma's grandmother had bought the place, when the previous owners had lived there.

"Yes," Emma nodded, "I might as well. I haven't got anything else to do."

"Watch the tide," said Samuel. "It can be treacherous this time o' year."

"Oh, I shan't go swimming," said Emma. "I'm not very good at swimming."

Samuel grunted and went back to his weeding and Emma carried on across the lawn towards a belt of hydrangea bushes. The bushes were so thick that the steep path that led down the cliff to the beach was almost hidden. Emma knew it was there because she'd come down here before on other occasions when she'd visited her grandmother.

There were steps at the end of the path, deep steps hewn out of the cliff and supported by strips of wood. At the bottom Emma slipped off her shoes and, leaving them on the last step, she jumped, landing heavily in the soft, pale sand.

It was quiet on the beach, the air so fresh that if Emma ran her tongue over her lips she could taste the salt. The only sounds were the cries of gulls as they swooped for food and the distant echo of a ship's horn far away on the horizon.

Emma shaded her eyes from the sun and wondered where the ship was going. China perhaps, or Singapore, where Dad was. She felt her throat tighten as it always did whenever she thought of her father.

Slowly she made her way across the beach, stumbling in the deep, dry sand that was already warm in spite of the earliness of the hour.

Where the dry sand ended and the vast expense of wet sand began there were small pools of water where the outgoing tide had become trapped by clusters of rocks.

Emma gasped as her feet touched the cold water then gave a little shiver as her toes sank into the sand. Crouching down she watched as a tiny, almost transparent crab darted across her feet only to become marooned on a clump of red seaweed drying on a rock. Emma picked up the seaweed, holding it between finger and thumb, before placing it in the pool where it became a mass of waving pink strands.

Emma, her earlier misery forgotten, watched fascinated as the crab scurried away. Then gradually, above the gentle swish of the waves and the cries of the sea birds, she became aware of another sound, the sound of voices and of laughter.

Looking along the beach to the far end where the cliffs were steeper, Emma could see a group of people. She stood up, frowning, wondering where they had come from, for she hadn't seen them arrive and they certainly hadn't passed her.

Maybe, she thought, they had been there all the time, but if they had it seemed strange that she hadn't noticed them. In fact, when she had jumped down the last step on to the sand Emma could have sworn the beach had been empty. Slowly she began to walk towards them.

A woman was spreading a tartan rug on the dry sand and had already set up a white sunshade. There were several children. Two of them, Emma could see, were little more than babies.

As Emma approached, the woman looked in her direction before turning her attention to the youngest of the children, who had crawled from the rug and appeared to be trying to eat the sand.

The older children, two boys and a girl, had run down to the wet sand where they were laughing and whooping and throwing a ball to each other, until one of the boys suddenly spotted Emma. He stopped and said something to the other two and they all stared in her direction.

The boy who had seen her first began to walk towards her and for some reason Emma suddenly felt nervous.

He was older than her, she thought, and as he grew closer she noticed his hair was dark and straight and he was wearing rather baggy shorts and a blue shirt with a white stripe round the collar. His clothes reminded Emma of something but for the moment she couldn't think what.

"Good morning," the boy said as he reached her. "I'm William Carstairs." He held out his hand. "Who are you?"

"Emma," said Emma, taking his outstretched hand, which felt warm and dry against her own damp one. "Emma Thornton." She felt a bit silly shaking hands with him. None of her friends shook hands. When he let go of her hand Emma found herself wiping her moist palms down the side of her pink shorts.

"Did you know this was a private beach?" asked the boy. He sounded curious, almost as if he was surprised at finding Emma there.

"Of course," Emma replied. "But my grandmother said I could come here." She was about to ask if the boy also had permission when he said,

"Who is your grandmother?"

"Mrs Cunningham," Emma replied. "She owns the hotel – The Seahorse Bay Hotel." She pointed back towards the pathway.

"Do you live there?" asked the boy.

"No, we..." Emma paused, then said, "Well yes, I suppose we do now."

The boy stared at her as if he didn't know quite what to say next; then as the other two children ran up, he said, "This is my sister, Charlotte." Emma found herself looking into a pair of black eyes that sparkled with mischief. "And my brother, Edward."

"Hello," said Emma, embarrassed again as she realized she was expected to shake hands with both children. The girl, Charlotte, Emma thought was about twelve, the same age as herself, while the boy, Edward, was a little younger and as fair as his brother and sister were dark. His eyes were as blue as the sea, his skin as pale as the tiny shells that lay on the sand. He was wearing identical clothing to his brother but still Emma couldn't think what the clothing reminded her of.

Charlotte wore a white dress with a pink ribbon threaded through the waistband. Emma thought she looked dressed more for a party instead of a trip to the beach.

"Is that your mother?" Emma turned and,

looking at the woman who was sitting down now on the tartan rug, thought she must be very hot. Her face was shaded from the sun by the brim of a straw hat but she was wearing a long-sleeved blouse and a skirt that reached her ankles.

"Oh no!" Charlotte giggled. "That is Nanny, she looks after—"

"The babies," interrupted William. "She looks after the babies." He turned and nodded towards the two younger children who were sitting beneath the sunshade. "Louise and George," he said.

"Do you live here?" asked Emma.

"Only some of the time," said Edward. "We live in London really."

"And some of the time our parents live in India," said William.

"My father lives in Singapore," said Emma.

The two boys looked at her with fresh interest. "Is that where you live some of the time?" asked William.

"Oh no," said Emma. "I've never been there. Mum and I live … used to live … in Milton Keynes."

"I've never heard of that," said Charlotte.

"It's quite a big place," said Emma defensively. She wasn't quite sure what else to say. "So where is your house?" she said at last, looking towards the cliffs at the far end of the beach. "The one you live in some of the time?"

"It's up there," said Edward, pointing. "It's hidden by the trees. Where is your hotel?"

"You can't see that either," said Emma. "It's over there." She pointed back the way she had come.

"We were going to play rounders," said William. "Would you like to play? You would even up the teams. I was going to have to play the other two on my own but you could be on my team."

"I'm not sure if I can play rounders," said Emma.

The children stared at her in astonishment. "I played it once," she said hastily, "but it was a long time ago and I don't think I remember how."

"What do you usually play on the beach?" asked Charlotte.

"The last time I came we played with a frisbee," said Emma, "but Dad was with us then..."

"What's a frisbee?" asked Edward.

"It's a sort of plate thing," said Emma, amazed that they didn't know, but at the same time secretly pleased that she knew something that these rather superior children didn't. "Like a flying saucer really."

William frowned. "Come on," he said. "We'll show you how to play rounders."

They played on the wet sand, the ridges formed by the tide hard beneath their bare feet. They used stones as posts and a piece of driftwood as a bat while the sun climbed higher in the sky, the gulls swooped and cried and the babies slept under the sunshade.

Charlotte, with her black hair streaming behind her and her long brown legs flying over the sand, to Emma's amazement outran them all. She had tucked her skirt into her pants, which Emma could not help but notice were edged with delicate white lace.

"We have a boat," said Edward later when the game was over and they were sitting on the hot dry sand and had given up trying to settle the argument over who had won. "It's up there in the house boat in the trees."

"It belongs to Albert really," said Charlotte, gathering up her damp hair on to the top of her head and securing it with a pretty butterfly-shaped hairslide.

"Who's Albert?" asked Emma, watching her and wishing her own straight fair hair was as long, and curled like Charlotte's did.

"Our brother," said Edward. "We're not allowed to get the boat out unless he is with us."

"It's time to go now," called a voice.

They all looked up and Emma saw that the woman with the straw hat had stood up and was beckoning to the children.

"Will you be here tomorrow?" William turned to Emma.

"Oh yes," she said, then, not wanting him to think she was too eager, she added, "I expect so."

"Goodbye," said William. "We have to go now."

Emma watched as they ran up the beach

and began to help with the sunshade, the tartan rug and the two babies. When at last they had packed everything up they trailed slowly to the far end of the beach where they disappeared one by one into what seemed to be an opening in the trees and gorse bushes.

Emma watched in amazement. There must be another pathway there, she thought, another pathway to the cliffs.

William was the last to go and just before he too disappeared from sight he turned and waved. Emma waved back then with a sigh she began to walk along the beach.

It wasn't until she'd nearly reached her own pathway that she remembered what her mother had said about not talking to strangers. But she wouldn't have meant the Carstairs family, thought Emma as she stopped to wipe the sand from between her toes and put on her shoes, they wouldn't really be what her mother meant by strangers...

But the more she thought about it the more Emma wondered if they hadn't been exactly what her mother meant. After all, there *had* been something rather strange about them.

She wasn't quite able to put her finger on what it was, but they had definitely been a bit odd.

On the other hand they had been nice, and they were going to be on the beach again the next day. With a sudden tingle of excitement Emma felt really happy for the first time since that dreadful morning when her mother had told her they had to move from their home in Milton Keynes.

Chapter 2

Emma made her way slowly up the path through the hydrangeas to the hotel grounds. Old Samuel Moses was clipping the edges of the lawn now with a pair of long-handled shears. He nodded when he saw Emma. She waved and carried on into the hotel where she found her mother in the kitchen preparing vegetables with Mrs Bates, the hotel cook.

"Oh, there you are," said Mum. "I was just wondering where you'd got to."

"I've been to the beach," said Emma. Leaning across the kitchen table she took a pea pod from the mound of vegetables in the centre. Snapping it open she hooked out the peas with her thumb then one by one popped them into her mouth.

"I expect you'll find it a bit lonely here," said Mrs Bates, turning from the larder where she had just taken a string of onions from a hook on the door. "There aren't too many children around here of your age," she added.

"Actually," said Emma, taking another pod and opening it, "I met some people on the beach."

"Did you?" Emma's mother looked up sharply.

"Yes," Emma nodded, "they were really nice. I played rounders with them."

"Were they on holiday?" asked Mrs Bates.

"Sort of," said Emma.

"Emma!" said Mum sharply as Emma reached out her hand for another pea pod. "Don't eat any more of those, there won't be any left for the evening meal."

"Sorry." Emma threw Mrs Bates a guilty glance but the cook didn't seem bothered by the loss of a few pea pods. She seemed more concerned about the people Emma had been playing with.

"Did they know it's a private beach?" she asked with a frown.

"Oh yes," said Emma. "In fact one of the boys told me it was private."

"I wonder who they were," said Mrs Bates. "Mrs Cunningham is very strict about visitors using the beach. Even hotel guests have to ask her permission first."

"Were their parents with them, Emma?" asked Mum, suddenly interested now, Emma thought, because Mrs Bates was making an issue of it.

"No." Emma shook her head. "They had an au pair girl with them. At least I suppose she was an au pair. Tamsin Jacobs had an au pair, didn't she, Mum?"

"Yes, dear, she did." Mum nodded.

"They still shouldn't have been on the beach, no matter who was with them," sniffed Mrs Bates. "Mrs Cunningham won't like it."

"Grandma won't know if we don't tell her," said Emma.

"Emma, that's not very nice!" Her mother looked shocked.

"Well, if she finds out, she might stop them

going on the beach," said Emma. "Then I won't have anyone to play with again."

"The Elliott family will be here soon," said Mrs Bates. "I expect you'll be able to play with them – they come from London," she added.

"So do the children I met," said Emma.

The kitchen phone rang at that moment and Mrs Bates hurried to answer it. Mum carried on preparing the vegetables and Emma, watching her, found herself wondering what would happen if her grandmother found out that not only did the Carstairs family use her beach, but that they also kept a boat down there as well.

She decided in the end it would be better to say nothing, even to her mother, at least for the time being.

She dreamt about her new friends that night. About Charlotte with her laughing black eyes and beautiful tumbling hair, about William with his serious smile, and Edward, shy Edward who looked as if a puff of wind could blow him away.

She dreamt she was running with them on the hard wet sand, her feet making imprints behind her. She dreamt they swam together in the sea, the surf crashing around them, until Old Samuel Moses called to them to come out, that it wasn't safe to swim there – that the tides could be dangerous.

Then she dreamt she sat beneath the white sunshade on the tartan rug with the babies, Louise and George, and the lady with the straw hat whose name she didn't know. The lady had a kind smile and thick brown hair coiled into a bun at the nape of her neck.

When she awoke the next morning Emma was happy. So happy that she didn't think about Lucy, or the new boy Simon, or any of her other friends that she had been forced to leave behind in Milton Keynes.

It was the first morning since coming to Seahorse Bay that she hadn't woken up thinking about them all, because this morning she had something else to think about.

She could hardly wait to get down to the beach after breakfast. She suddenly had the awful feeling that William, Charlotte and

Edward might not be there. That because she had dreamt about them the night before that maybe she had also dreamt about meeting them in the first place, that somehow they didn't really exist, were just in her imagination.

But as soon as she stepped on to the warm sand Emma knew she need not have worried, for one glance along the beach told her all she needed to know.

The tide was far out again and Charlotte, her skirt tucked above her knees, was paddling in the shallow water. William and Edward were bending over a green painted rowing boat that had been dragged down to the water's edge and the au pair girl was sitting beneath the sunshade on the same tartan rug with the two younger children.

Emma felt her throat tighten with excitement and as she started forward across the sand Charlotte looked up, saw her, waved excitedly and called out to the two boys. They too looked up and waved.

"We hoped you would come," said Edward as Emma, breathless from running across the sand, reached them. "We're going out in the boat later, we wondered if you would like to come with us."

"Oh." Emma stopped and looked at the boat. "I don't know," she said, wondering what her mother would say, and come to that what her grandmother would say.

"It's all right," said Edward. "Albert will be coming with us."

"I could manage the boat without Albert," said William with a sniff.

"I think I should ask my mother first," said Emma then curiously, thinking it could probably make a difference, said, "How old is Albert exactly?"

"Albert's nineteen," called Charlotte, who had run out of the water to join them and who must have heard what they had been saying.

"There are a lot of you, aren't there?" said Emma wistfully. "I wish I had lots of brothers and sisters."

"We have another sister as well," said Charlotte.

Emma stared at her.

"Olivia is twenty." Charlotte tossed her

head and Emma saw she was wearing the same butterfly hairslide that she had worn the day before. "She is getting engaged," Charlotte went on, "and when she gets married she said I will be a bridesmaid."

"I was a bridesmaid once," said Emma, "to my auntie."

"So are you going to go and ask your mother if you can come out with us in the boat?" asked William. He sounded impatient, as if he was bored with the talk of weddings and bridesmaids.

"She needn't go yet," said Charlotte. "Albert won't be here for ages. Besides, I want to play rounders again before the tide comes in."

Charlotte got her way and soon they were all involved in another fast and furious game of rounders.

It wasn't until the sea began to inch its way up the beach and lap around the edges of the green painted boat that Edward finally flung himself on to the dry sand. "I can't play any more," he gasped. "I'm puffed out."

They sat for a while recovering their breath

and Emma couldn't remember the last time she had enjoyed herself as much.

"I'd better go and ask about the boat," she said at last, scrambling to her feet, "just in case your brother arrives."

The others nodded.

"I won't be long," she said. "Don't go without me." Then she sped off along the beach.

By the time she reached the hotel she was completely out of breath. Her mother wasn't in the garden, the dining-room, or the lounge and when in desperation Emma burst into the kitchen she found only Mrs Bates there making pastry.

"They've gone to the Cash 'n' Carry." Mrs Bates looked at Emma, her rolling pin poised in the air above the sheet of pastry. "I told your mother I would give you your lunch."

"Oh no!" said Emma in dismay.

"Something wrong, love?" asked Mrs Bates.

"I wanted to ask Mum if I could go out in the boat with my friends."

"Boat?" Mrs Bates frowned and draped the

pastry over a pie dish packed with fruit. "Well, I don't know about that, I'm sure."

"D'you think she would let me go?" asked Emma anxiously.

"Well, your mum might," said Mrs Bates, "but I don't know about your gran. She doesn't even know about these new friends of yours, does she?"

"No." Emma shook her head.

"And as for going out in a boat... What are they doing with a boat down there anyway? Are they Sea Scouts or something?"

"Sea Scouts?" Emma stared at Mrs Bates.

"Yes, my niece's boys are in the local Sea Scouts – they have a boat."

Something had clicked in Emma's mind and she suddenly knew that was what William and Edward's clothes had reminded her of, some sort of uniform – maybe that was it – the Sea Scouts.

"Mind you," Mrs Bates carried on, "even if they are Sea Scouts I wouldn't imagine your grandmother would be too pleased about them using her private beach. I really don't know, I'm sure... I think you'll just have to wait until they get back."

"But they may be ages!" wailed Emma. "My friends will have gone by then."

"Well, I'm sorry, love," said Mrs Bates, lifting the pie dish and cutting the pastry carefully from the side with a sharp knife. "It really isn't for me to say, you know. Maybe you'll be able to go with them another time."

"But I want to go today," said Emma.

"All you can do is hope your mum will be back soon," said Mrs Bates.

With a deep sigh Emma flopped down on to a kitchen stool. No one understood. No one had really known how she'd felt having to leave her friends and now she'd made new friends, it seemed everyone was being as difficult as they could.

With her elbows on the table and her chin in her hands she gloomily watched the second hand on the kitchen clock as it went round and round.

"So what's the name of these new friends of yours?" asked Mrs Bates after she'd put her pie in the oven and was clearing up the scraps of pastry.

"Carstairs," replied Emma. "William, Charlotte and Edward Carstairs."

"And you say they are on holiday here?"

"Yes," she nodded. "Well, I think so, they said they live here some of the time and in London the rest of the time."

"What was the name again?" Mrs Bates frowned.

"Carstairs," said Emma. "Do you know them?" she added eagerly.

Mrs Bates shook her head. "No, never heard of them. But your grandmother won't like them using the beach, I can tell you that for a fact."

"Why doesn't Grandma like other people going on the beach?" asked Emma after a moment.

"Well, because it's private," said Mrs Bates. "It belongs to her."

"Yes, I know," said Emma, "but I just wondered if she had a reason, that's all... Grandma's usually kind to people..."

"She's probably thinking of what happened there in the past," said Mrs Bates darkly.

"What do you mean?" Emma looked up

quickly. "What did happen there in the past?"

"Oh, it was donkey's years ago but the locals say there was a child drowned in the bay once – a young boy I believe."

"Samuel said it was dangerous to swim there," Emma said.

"Yes, well," said Mrs Bates, "he would know. He's been around longer than anyone."

Emma spent the next hour in an agony of suspense waiting for her mother to return.

"I wanted to ask you something," she said accusingly when at last her mother came into the kitchen laden with boxes and cartons.

"It sounds important," said Mum, laughing.

"It is," said Emma. " I wanted to know if I could go out in a boat."

"A boat?" Her mother looked startled.

"Yes, with my new friends," said Emma, glancing at the clock, suddenly hopeful again that it might not be too late. "It would be all right," she added quickly when she caught sight of her mother's doubtful expression, "their brother would be with them, and he's nineteen. Can I, Mum? Can I go?"

"I don't know, Emma." Mum sounded worried. "I really don't know. These new friends of yours may be very nice but we can't get away from the fact that they are using Grandma's private beach without her permission. And you say now they even have a boat as well?"

Emma stared at her mother in dismay. She knew that tone of voice. She'd heard it before. It usually meant a definite no was coming.

"Will you come down there with me?" she said, desperately saying the first thing that came into her head. "Come and meet them, then you can see for yourself just how nice they are."

Still Mum hesitated.

"Please, Mum," said Emma, "please."

Her mother glanced at the kitchen clock. "All right," she said at last, and Emma breathed a sigh of relief. "But we'll have to be quick, I have work to do."

"That's OK." Emma jumped from the stool. "We will have to be quick anyway, otherwise they will have gone."

Emma hurried so fast down the path to the

beach that her mother almost had to run to keep up with her, but when she jumped the last steep step on to the sand she gave a cry of dismay.

"Oh, they've gone!" she said, looking along the empty stretch of beach.

The tide had come in and almost reached the dry sand. Not only was there no sign of William, Charlotte, Edward or the green painted boat, but the sunshade had also been taken down and the au pair girl and the two babies had gone.

Mum shaded her eyes and looked out to sea. "I can't see a boat," she said, "only those yachts right out on the horizon."

"They didn't wait..." said Emma in disappointment.

"Never mind," said Mum kindly. "Maybe I'll meet them another day. Come on, Emma, we'd best get back now. Perhaps we'll go out this evening, maybe into Sandcoombe and walk along the pier. Would you like that?"

"If you like," said Emma with a shrug and a last look along the deserted beach.

But they didn't go out that evening for

when they got back to the hotel it was to find that while they had been at the beach the Elliott family had arrived from London.

Chapter 3

There were three Elliott children. Jason, a thin boy of twelve who wore a red base-ball cap, his eleven-year-old sister Kylie, and Charlene who was eight. Both Kylie and Charlene had lots of freckles and hair the colour of conkers. The family's Range Rover, complete with trailer and a rubber dinghy with an outboard motor, was parked on the drive in front of the hotel.

"Maybe Mr Elliott will take you for a ride in their boat," said Mum later that evening.

Emma wasn't sure she would want to go even if Mr Elliott asked her. She would much rather go in the green painted boat that belonged to the Carstairs family with their brother Albert at the oars.

In fact by the end of that first evening Emma knew she wasn't going to like the Elliott children half as much as she liked the Carstairs.

"Do you live here?" asked Kylie in a contemptuous sort of voice as they sat together on the swing-seat in the garden watching Jason kick his football against the wall.

"We do now," said Emma, wishing she could go to her room.

"Why?" said Kylie with a sly smile, almost as if she knew that Emma didn't really want to talk about it.

"Because my parents are getting divorced," said Emma, hoping that would shut her up, "and my grandma said we could come and live with her."

"Oh," said Kylie. Then she seemed to think about it for a while before she said, "There's not much to do here, is there?"

"I thought that at first," said Emma. "But I was wrong."

"My mum and dad want to come here to

live," said Kylie, "but I would hate it if they did. I know I would."

"Oi!" A sudden shout made both girls look up. Old Samuel Moses was thundering across the lawn shaking his fist at Jason, who had kicked his football into the dahlia bed.

Jason fled without even retrieving his ball while old Samuel picked up several broken dahlias and stood there shaking his head and looking at them with tears in his eyes.

"I'm going in," said Kylie, jumping off the swing-seat, probably afraid that she would get the blame for the damage her brother had caused. "I'll see you in the morning," she called over her shoulder as she walked across the lawn to the hotel, "then you can show me what there is to do here."

Emma didn't want to show Kylie or her awful brother anything and by the next morning she had already made up her mind to keep out of their way. While the Elliott family were still at breakfast in the dining-room she attempted to slip away. With a bit of luck, she thought, the Carstairs children might already be on the beach.

She was just creeping under the dining-room windows when a voice suddenly made her jump.

"What are you doing?"

Emma looked up sharply to find Kylie not in the dining-room as she had thought but sitting on the wall watching her.

Feeling both guilty and rather silly Emma straightened up. "I'm going to the beach," she said.

"I'll come with you." Kylie jumped off the wall.

"Aren't you supposed to be eating your breakfast?" asked Emma desperately.

"I hate breakfast," said Kylie.

"Oh," said Emma, then even more desperately, she said, "but what about your brother and your sister, won't they wonder where you are?"

If she had thought that might deter Kylie she was mistaken, for the girl simply lifted her head and at the top of her voice yelled, "Ja...son! Char...lene!"

The sound of clattering chairs came through the open dining-room windows and seconds later Jason came running around the side of the hotel followed by Charlene.

"We're going to the beach," Kylie told them. "With her," she nodded towards Emma.

Before Emma had the chance to protest the children's mother appeared at the open dining-room window. "Where are you going?" she asked.

"To the beach," said Jason. "With her – Emma," he added.

Emma gazed at Mrs Elliott, willing her to say they couldn't go, but to her dismay her own mother suddenly appeared. "They'll be all right," she said. "Emma likes to play on the beach."

"Oh good," said Mrs Elliott. "We'll leave the children here while we go into Sandcoombe for some shopping."

Emma, close now to despair, stared at her mother, who said, "Off you go, dear. Have a nice time. Maybe your other friends will be there today."

"What other friends?" asked Jason as they made their way down the path to the beach.

"A family who are staying in a house on the cliffs," said Emma coolly.

"How many children are there?" asked Kylie.

"Five," replied Emma, then after a moment's thought added, "well, there are seven really, but two are much older and two still babies."

"Seven!" Kylie stared at her. "I don't believe you. No one has seven children."

"Well, they have," retorted Emma. "You'll see in a minute."

"Are there any boys?" asked Jason.

"Yes, there are William and Edward and..." She was going to say, "and George the baby, and Albert," but Jason interrupted her.

"Are they older than me?" he asked warily.

"William is," Emma replied, "and bigger, much bigger, and so is Albert – he's nineteen." The fact that she hadn't even met Albert didn't worry Emma at that moment.

Jason was silent after that until they reached the beach, then he stopped and looked round. "So where are they then, these friends of yours?" he asked suspiciously.

Emma shaded her eyes and scanned the

entire length of the beach right up to the rocks around the distant headland, but it was deserted with not a soul in sight. Only the ever-hungry gulls swooped and screamed overhead.

"They're not here yet," she said, "but they will be soon."

"So what's there to do around here?" Jason, with his hands on his hips, stood and surveyed the scene: the soft, dry sand already warm from the morning sun; the acres of hard wet sand; the rock pools; and the shimmering band of the sea. "It looks dead boring to me," he said.

"No, it isn't," said Emma indignantly, "there's lots to do."

"Like what?" said Kylie, her lip curling.

"Yeah, like what?" echoed Charlene.

"I s'pose we could swim," said Jason.

"We're not allowed to," said Emma quickly. "Not from this beach."

"Why not?" demanded Kylie.

"Because it's dangerous. Mrs Bates, our cook at the hotel, said that a boy once drowned in this bay."

"He couldn't have been a very good swimmer," said Jason. "I'm an excellent swimmer."

"Maybe you'd better not though, Jas," said Kylie doubtfully.

"We could climb those cliffs." Jason, looking around, pointed to the cliffs at the very end of the bay. "I bet there are birds' nests on those cliffs."

"I shouldn't think my grandmother would let anyone do that either," said Emma.

"Oh, for goodness' sake!" Jason exploded. "So what can we do! It's like I said, dead boring!" He began kicking at a piece of cuttlefish with the toe of his trainers, embedding it more deeply in the sand.

"No, it isn't," said Emma again, "there's lots to do."

"What do you do with these other friends of yours?" asked Kylie.

"We play rounders," said Emma.

"What's rounders?" asked Charlene.

"It's a stupid game," scoffed Jason.

"No, it isn't," said Emma hotly.

"Well, we can't play it," retorted Jason,

"because you need a bat and posts for rounders."

"We use stones for posts and..." Emma looked round, her eye coming to rest on the piece of driftwood they had used the day before, "and that piece of wood for a bat..." she went on.

"That's stupid," said Jason, "you can't play without a proper bat. Besides we haven't even got a ball with us and if I don't get my football back from that loony old gardener—"

"He's not loony," retorted Emma. "Anyway, the others have got a ball," she added. "They'll be here soon. It'll be fun. There'll be enough of us today for two proper teams."

"I don't want to play rounders," said Charlene.

"Neither do I," said Kylie. "It sounds a really silly game. And let's face it, Emma, it doesn't look as if your friends are coming, does it?"

"They will," said Emma stoutly. "Of course they will. I expect they'll be taking their boat out again like they did yesterday."

Jason looked up quickly. "What sort of boat

have they got?" he said. "Is it like ours?"

"No." Emma frowned and shook her head. "No, not really."

"Is it a powerboat?" Jason's eyes widened.

"No..."

"So, is it a yacht?" he persisted.

Emma shook her head. "No," she said, "it's green, and it has oars."

"A rowing boat!" scoffed Jason. "Is that all? They sound a weird lot, these friends of yours. They use a piece of wood instead of a bat and ride around in a rowing boat. Doesn't it even have an outboard motor?"

"D'you know what I think?" said Kylie suddenly. "I think there's no such thing as these weird friends of Emma's. I think she made them up."

"Don't be ridiculous!" cried Emma hotly. "Of course I didn't. You'll see, they'll be here in a minute."

But the minutes ticked by and the Carstairs didn't come.

Jason hurled pebbles into the sea, trying to make them bounce on the waves, growing bored when they didn't.

Kylie sat down on the sand declaring that she was hot and demanding to know why this silly beach didn't have ice-creams like every other beach she'd been on.

Charlene wandered off to look into a rock pool then began screaming when a crab nipped her toe.

"I'm bored," said Jason, flinging one last pebble into the sea. "I'm going back to the hotel." He began running up the beach and after a moment Kylie and Charlene began to trail after him.

Emma watched them go then sat down on the dry sand to wait for her friends. But still they didn't come and at last with one, final, wistful look along the deserted beach, Emma reluctantly decided she too should go back to the hotel.

The following morning as the Elliott family were leaving the dining-room Mr Elliott called out to Emma, who was helping her mother to clear the tables.

"Would you like to come out in our boat with us?" he asked.

Before Emma could answer her mother looked up and said, "Well, that's very kind of you, Mr Elliott, I'm sure Emma would love to, wouldn't you, Emma?"

Still without giving Emma a chance to reply, Mr Elliott said, "Right, we'll be going in about half an hour, Emma. Meet us outside. Don't worry –" he looked at Emma's mother again – "we have a spare life jacket, she'll be quite safe."

"Oh, I'm sure she will," said Mum. "Like I said, it's very kind of you to ask her. I worry that Emma hasn't got company of her own age."

Jason grinned at Emma as he passed her. "See you later," he said. "Don't be late. This way you get to have a ride in a proper boat."

Emma scowled after him and angrily pulled a tablecloth off one of the tables.

"Well, that's nice, dear, isn't it?" said Mum, turning to Emma as the dining-room door closed behind the Elliotts. "It'll make up for missing your boat ride yesterday."

"No, it won't," said Emma stubbornly. "Nothing will."

"But...?" Mum looked bewildered.

"I don't want to go," said Emma.

"I thought you would jump at it," said Mum.

"You didn't even ask me if I wanted to go," Emma muttered.

"Honestly, Emma!" Mum sounded exasperated now. "I just don't understand you sometimes. Anyway, you'll have to go now. It will seem very rude if you don't."

Emma didn't reply but after she'd finished the tables she changed into jeans and a sweatshirt and went out to the front of the hotel where she found the Elliotts piling themselves into their Range Rover.

Emma sat in the back seat between Kylie and Charlene and as Mr Elliott switched on the engine he glanced over his shoulder and said, "We'll go down to the harbour in Sandcoombe then take a trip out to Brandon Point."

"Oh brilliant," said Jason, "that's miles away."

The harbour was busy with fishing boats, and day trippers arriving by ferry, while yachts glided in and out of the smart new marina.

Mrs Elliott fitted Emma with her life jacket and in spite of the fact that Emma hadn't wanted to go, as they took their places in the dinghy and chugged out of the harbour she felt a tingle of excitement.

Within moments they had rounded the headland and were soon streaking across the sparkling water bouncing up and down as the dinghy hit the waves.

Jason, who was at the front of the boat with his father, turned and looked at Emma. "Better than a stupid old rowing boat, isn't it?" he laughed. He was wearing his baseball cap back to front and Emma thought he looked really silly, but she was saved from having to answer by Mrs Elliott, who suddenly touched her arm.

"Look," she said, pointing, "there's Seahorse Bay. You can see the hotel up there on the cliffs."

Emma craned her neck. The Seahorse Bay Hotel looked very different from this angle with its green tiled roof glittering in the sun and its white walls surrounded by the mass of pink and blue hydrangeas. Her gaze moved along the clifftop. Surely from here she should be able to see the other house, the house where the Carstairs family were staying.

Carefully she scanned the clifftops but the trees at the opposite end of the bay from the hotel grew so close together that all that was visible from the sea was a dense expanse of foliage, while below, the beach itself was still deserted.

"I still reckon I could climb those cliffs," Jason suddenly boasted.

"Don't even think of it," said his father. "There's a skill to rock climbing."

Emma hardly heard what they were saying for she was still staring at the empty beach and wondering why her friends seemed to have stopped going there.

Then as Mr Elliott turned the dinghy in the direction of the distant Brandon Point Emma made up her mind what she would do. When she got back to the hotel, while the Elliotts were having their dinner, she would go to the beach, and if the Carstairs children weren't there this time, she would go and find them.

Chapter 4

They weren't there, but Emma hadn't really thought they would be.

It was a calm, still evening, the tide was out and the sea looked like glass. A light mist hovered, hiding the horizon, and a ship far out in the bay looked as if it was sailing through the sky.

Emma took off her shoes and hurried along the beach to the far end. The entrance to the pathway was almost hidden by overhanging gorse and broom, while the path itself was even steeper than the one to the hotel.

It was dark and rather creepy with the trees on either side meeting overhead.

It was also very quiet, the only sound that

of the sea, and Emma, hurrying through the tunnel of trees looking neither to the right nor to the left, was relieved when she finally reached the top.

There was a patch of bright sunlight at the end of the path and a white gate that stood open swinging gently on its hinges. Emma stopped at the gate and stared at the top bar which had a name painted on it in black lettering.

She traced the letters with her finger. Darbhanga ... a strange name. She was just wondering what it meant when she happened to glance up, and as she caught her first glimpse of the house, all other thoughts flew from her mind.

It was a very large house, three storeys high with balconies at the upper windows. Bathed in the glow from the last rays of the setting sun it looked pink.

A glass-roofed veranda surrounded the ground floor and soft velvet lawns spread all the way from the house to the top of the cliffs. Tall fir trees guarded the building, casting long shadows across the grass.

Slowly Emma started to walk towards the house and as she drew closer she could see there were cane tables and chairs on the veranda while behind the tall windows, lace curtains fluttered in a sudden gentle breeze.

A woman stepped out of the French doors, not the au pair girl who had been with the children, but a tall woman with her hair piled high on the top of her head. She was wearing a long, pale blue dress and as Emma stopped, the woman turned and looked in her direction.

Emma held her breath and, suddenly afraid the woman would catch sight of her and want to know what she was doing, she crouched down behind a large rhododendron bush.

The woman looked away again and at that moment, to Emma's delight, Charlotte and William came out of the house. She wanted to run forward then to tell them she was there, but something stopped her, and instead she remained hidden behind the bushes.

The woman leaned against the veranda rail and seemed to be talking to Charlotte, then she laughed and, slipping one arm around

Charlotte's shoulders, turned as if to go back into the house.

Then the woman paused, lingered for a moment in the doorway and said something to William. He shook his head in reply and after they had gone, he sat down in one of the cane chairs.

When Emma saw that William was alone she slipped out from behind the bushes and tiptoed across the grass.

The dew had already begun to form and Emma's toes became quite wet. She reached the veranda without William noticing her, then in a loud whisper, she called his name.

Sharply he turned his head and when he caught sight of her, his eyes widened in amazement.

"Emma!" He gasped and jumped to his feet.

"Hello, William." Suddenly she felt shy.

In a flash he was down the veranda steps and at her side. "What are you doing here?" he asked.

"I came to find you," she replied. "You haven't been at the beach and I wondered if everything was all right."

William stared at her for a moment then he glanced over his shoulder. "Let's walk," he said.

"But what about Charlotte...?" Emma glanced up at the house. "Can I see Charlotte...?"

"Charlotte's gone to change for dinner," he said. "My parents and my sister and her fiancé are here from London. We are celebrating their engagement. It's all been pretty hectic, that's why we haven't been to the beach."

"Oh," said Emma. "Oh, I see. I thought something might be wrong."

"No," said William. "No, there is nothing wrong at all. Far from it. In fact, it's like one long party at the moment." He paused. "I say, Emma, would you care to join us?"

"Me?" Emma looked startled. It had been one thing coming to find her new friends, it was quite another being asked to join them for dinner and what looked like a party.

"Yes, why not?" asked William enthusiastically. "I'm sure my mother wouldn't mind..."

"Oh, no really," said Emma, "it's kind of

you but I've already had my dinner."

"Have you?" William looked surprised.

"Yes, I had my dinner with Mrs Bates," said Emma. "And besides..." she glanced down at her jeans and T-shirt then at the smart evening suit William was wearing and trailed off. She had been about to say that she didn't feel dressed for a party but that seemed silly somehow because most parties she went to – usually barbecues or discos – she wore jeans anyway. Instead, she said, "Will you be at the beach tomorrow?"

"We may be," said William. "My sister Olivia likes the beach. She has persuaded everyone to go moonlight swimming later this evening. That is," he glanced at the sky, "if there's a moon."

Emma stared at him. "Do you mean swimming in the bay?" she asked anxiously and when William nodded, she went on quickly, "You do know it can be dangerous in the bay, don't you?"

"Dangerous?" William frowned. "What do you mean?" He smiled then. "Sharks and things?"

"No, not sharks." Emma laughed. "Something to do with tides, Mrs Bates said so."

"Who is this Mrs Bates?" William was frowning again but he still had a half smile on his face.

"She's our cook."

"Oh, I see." He nodded. "Well, what did she say?"

"She said a boy drowned in the bay a long time ago. That it isn't safe to swim there."

"We haven't heard that story," said William. "But don't worry, we'll be careful."

By this time they had reached the white gate on the far side of the lawn. William stopped and looked back at the house. "I really should go in," he said, "we have guests arriving." He said it reluctantly, as if he didn't really want to go, as if he wanted to stay there and talk to Emma.

Emma was pleased and she also wished he didn't have to go.

"Are you sure you won't come inside?" he said wistfully.

Emma turned and looked back at the house. Other figures had appeared on the veranda and even from that distance Emma could see they were dressed in very fine clothes.

She wondered if it was a fancy dress party and was about to ask William, when he said, "We'll try and come to the beach tomorrow. But I must go now."

"All right." Emma nodded.

"Goodbye, Emma." He smiled again, then with one backward glance he was gone, striding swiftly across the lawn to the big house.

"Bye, William..." Emma watched as he reached the house then he bounded on to the veranda and disappeared inside.

The sun had set whilst they had been talking and with the deepening of the shadows, lights had come on inside the house and along the top of the veranda while others, hidden within the shrubbery, glowed softly.

Strains of music drifted across the lawns and with a sigh Emma turned and passed through the white gate.

Taking a deep breath she held it and hurried through the darkened tunnel of trees and down the steep pathway to the beach.

There had been so many things she'd wanted to say to William and she'd hardly said any of them. She'd meant to tell him about the awful Elliott children, had meant to ask if it was a fancy dress party they were having, and she'd meant to say she was sorry she'd been late for the boat ride ... but there had been no time.

Maybe tomorrow, she thought, as she made her way across the deserted beach.

She had just entered the hotel grounds when Kylie suddenly jumped out of the bushes in front of her. "Where have you been?" she demanded curiously.

"It's none of your business," said Emma.

"Your mum's been looking for you," said Kylie. "And your gran," she added triumphantly.

Emma didn't answer. She already knew she would be in trouble for going off without saying where she was going, she didn't need Kylie reminding her of that.

Kylie fell into step beside her and they crossed the lawn. "So where have you been?" Kylie asked again a moment later.

"To the beach," replied Emma abruptly, hoping that would keep her quiet.

"You haven't," said Kylie. "I know, because I went to look. The beach was empty. There was no one down there."

Emma was silent for a moment, then she said, "If you must know, I went to see my friends."

"That family with all the children?" asked Kylie curiously.

Emma nodded.

"So, did you see them?"

"Yes."

"I don't believe you," said Kylie.

"Well, I did. At least," Emma hesitated, "I saw William. I saw Charlotte too, but not to speak to."

"Is he your boyfriend, this William?" asked Kylie with her sly little smile.

"Of course not," Emma retorted, but she felt her cheeks grow hot.

"So where did you see him?" asked Kylie. By this time they had reached the hotel and they stopped for a moment on the terrace before going inside.

"At his house," replied Emma.

"You went to his house?" Kylie's eyes widened. "What will your mum say about that?"

"She wouldn't mind," said Emma. "Anyway, she won't know. Not unless you tell her."

"Where does he live then?"

"Quite near here actually." Emma didn't really know why she was telling Kylie all this. "It's a beautiful house further along the cliffs," she added.

"Will you take me there?" asked Kylie suddenly, unexpectedly.

"Why?" demanded Emma.

"Because I really would like to meet these mysterious friends of yours."

"Why do you call them mysterious?" Emma stared at her. "They're not mysterious at all."

"It seems funny we never get to see them," said Kylie. "Like I said before, I think you made them up."

"Don't be stupid," said Emma. "Of course I didn't make them up. And just to prove it, you can come to the beach with me tomorrow. They will be there then, and you can see for yourself."

"Good," said Kylie. "I'll look forward to it." She grinned over her shoulder at Emma then ran ahead into the hotel.

Later that night when Emma went to bed she stood for a moment at the open bedroom window. A huge moon surrounded by hundreds of stars hung in the sky and as she gazed up, Emma wished she could be on the beach with the swimming party.

She had half had it in mind to ask her mother if she could go and watch, but her mother hadn't been too happy about her disappearance after dinner, so Emma didn't think she would take too kindly to the idea.

In the end she'd kept quiet, consoling herself with the thought that she would see them all the next day on the beach, even if it did mean the awful Elliotts being there as well.

Chapter 5

The next morning there was no sign of Jason or Kylie, and Emma was just thinking she might sneak off to the beach on her own when her mother called her.

"Emma," she said, "I would like you to come into Sandcoombe with me this morning. I have to go to the bank for Grandma and we need to get ourselves registered with a local doctor and dentist."

"Do I have to go?" said Emma.

"Well, yes, I would like you to come with me," replied Mum, then staring closely at her, she said, "Why, what else did you want to do?"

"Nothing much," Emma shrugged. "I was only going to the beach."

"You can do that when we get back," said Mum. "Besides, we shouldn't be long."

Emma knew there was no use arguing, not when her mother had that certain look on her face.

There was still no sign of the Elliott family or their Range Rover when Emma and her mother left the hotel, but when they got to town they met Mr and Mrs Elliott and Charlene coming out of the pharmacy.

Mrs Elliott looked surprised to see Emma.

"Oh," she said, "Jason and Kylie have gone to the beach – they said they were going with you – they didn't want to come with us today."

"They'll be all right," said Emma's mother, "and we won't be long. We have a few things to do then Emma will be going back to the beach."

Emma suddenly felt sick. For some reason which she was unable to explain, she didn't want Jason and Kylie meeting the Carstairs family without her being there.

By now, probably that was exactly what had happened.

When they got back to the hotel Emma left her mother and hurried down the path to the beach.

She half expected to find Jason and Kylie playing rounders on the wet sand with the Carstairs children, that in some way they would have taken over, showing off, and boasting about their boat.

But to her surprise the beach was deserted and the tide was coming in with only the soft, dry sand visible where the sea never reached.

Emma stood for a while with the sand burning her toes, wondering what she should do.

Maybe she should simply go up to the big house again.

Something told her, however, that might not be such a good idea.

Reluctantly, she was about to turn away to go back to the hotel when she heard a faint noise.

It sounded like a shout, and it came from the far end of the beach.

Emma screwed up her eyes and, shielding them from the sun, she saw, in the distance, on the rocks beneath the cliffs, a bright splash of green.

She began to walk along the beach, stumbling a little in the deep dry sand, but it wasn't until she was much closer that it dawned on her that there was a figure on the rocks, and that the splash of colour she could see was a bright green T-shirt.

Emma wasn't sure at what point she realized that the figure was Kylie, because almost immediately the discovery was followed by a further shock when she caught sight of Jason halfway up the cliff face.

By this time Emma had almost reached the cliffs and she saw that the tide was already lapping at the edge of the rocks. Cupping her hands around her mouth she shouted to Kylie.

"Come back to the beach," she called, "you'll be cut off by the tide."

"I'm not leaving Jason," Kylie shouted back. "And he's stuck, he can't move."

Emma looked up at Jason who was clinging in terror to the cliff face.

"I'll go back for help," she called.

"No," Kylie shrieked. "Don't leave us! Come and help us!"

Emma hesitated. Really, she knew, she should go back to the hotel and get help, but by the time help arrived, it could be too late, the sea could have covered the rock where Kylie stood. And by then Jason may have lost his hold on the cliff face.

Swiftly she made up her mind and began scrambling over the rocks, slipping and sliding on green seaweed, scraping and twisting her ankles as she went. Maybe, if she was really quick, she could help them.

It took her a time, but eventually Emma reached Kylie who was sitting now, on a flat-tish rock, sobbing and hugging her knees.

"It's OK, Kylie," gasped Emma as anxiously she looked up at Jason directly above her.

He didn't seem to have moved a muscle.

"Jason," she shouted, "you must try to climb down."

Still he didn't move or speak.

"You must, Jason," sobbed Kylie, "or we'll all be drowned."

Between them they pleaded with Jason for

what seemed like hours until at last Emma turned again and saw to her horror that the tide had crept in even further.

The rocks, the cliff face and the headland were now all cut off from the beach.

"We're trapped!" she gasped. "Kylie, we're trapped!"

Wildly Kylie began to shout and scream, and after a while, Emma joined in.

Jason continued to cling in silence to the cliff face while the sea swirled and foamed around the rocks and the gulls swooped overhead.

Emma was just beginning to think all was lost and that they really would drown, when Kylie suddenly shrieked again and pointed out to sea. "Look!" she screamed. "Oh, look!"

Emma turned sharply and was in time to see the green rowing boat as it slid silently into view around the headland.

William and Charlotte were in the boat, together with a young man who pulled strongly at the oars and whom Emma, in spite of her terror, guessed must be Albert.

While William took the oars and held the boat steady, Albert slipped into the water, which almost reached his chest, and waded to the rocks.

"We will soon have you safe and dry," he said to Emma and Kylie.

In spite of the urgency of the moment Emma noticed that Albert looked like William, except that he was bigger and that he had a dark moustache.

He first lifted Kylie from the rocks and carried her through the water to the boat where Charlotte helped to pull her aboard. Then he returned for Emma.

As Albert told her to put her arms round his neck, she leaned against him in utter relief.

She really had thought they were going to drown and she could hardly believe they were actually being rescued.

Charlotte helped her as she scrambled from Albert's arms into the boat then, when she was sitting safely beside Kylie, Charlotte draped a rug around them both – a tartan rug – and Albert turned to go back through the sea for Jason.

By this time the water reached his shoulders and he was forced to swim.

Emma found herself holding her breath in terror as she watched, while beside her, Kylie sobbed and hiccupped.

Albert climbed out of the water on to the flat-topped rock, where only moments before the two girls had been sitting, and shouted up to Jason who was still clinging to the cliff.

They saw Jason look down, but still he didn't move.

Then, Albert began to climb the cliff face.

"Oh," gasped Kylie, "what's he going to do?"

"Don't worry," said William, turning his head to watch as he held the oars, "if anyone can get him down it will be Albert."

They all watched as Albert gripped Jason's ankles and began guiding his feet on to lower footholds.

The waves had started to wash over the rock by the time Jason finally reached it. At last, Albert swam back to the boat with Jason clinging to him, piggy-back style.

William rowed them back to the beach and

Jason sat shivering in the bottom of the boat with his teeth chattering.

Emma felt sorry for him but at the same time couldn't help thinking this just might teach him a lesson. He had after all been warned about climbing the cliffs, not only by her, but by his own father.

Albert and William drew the boat up on to the beach then helped them out on to the sand.

"Where do you live?" asked Albert, staring curiously at all three of them as they stood there shivering.

It was Charlotte who answered her brother's question, "Up there," she said, pointing towards the path to the hotel.

It was the first time Charlotte had spoken and Emma threw her a quick glance. It was then that she noticed how different Charlotte looked.

Her face was as white as chalk, her eyes red as if she'd been crying, and without their usual wicked look of amusement. Even her hair looked straggly, as if she hadn't even bothered to comb it that morning.

Emma was about to ask her if she was all right when Albert spoke again.

"We will have to leave you here," he said. "Will you be all right now?"

Emma nodded. "Yes … yes … th … thank you," she stuttered.

They watched as Albert and William began to push the boat into the water again.

William jumped in and it was then that Emma saw there was something different about him as well. She hadn't noticed it before, while they were being rescued, because she had been so terrified, but now that the danger was past, she couldn't help but see the difference.

William was grim-faced and unsmiling and when Albert finally waded into the water and jumped into the boat, taking his place at the oars once more, neither he nor Charlotte looked up.

"Thank you…" called Emma.

William did look back then, and gave her a half-smile. But it was a sad smile and it didn't reach his eyes.

She watched as the boat drew away with

Albert pulling strongly at the oars, Charlotte sitting hunched with her arms around her, and William staring out to sea.

"Em ... Emma..." stammered Kylie, breaking the silence. "Sh ... shall we g ... go back now...?"

Emma turned, still puzzled by the Carstairs' behaviour. "Yes, all right," she said.

It was a very subdued, silent little band that made its way up the steep cliff pathway.

When they reached the top it was Kylie who broke the silence.

"Don't tell anyone, Emma," she said urgently as they began to trail across the lawn.

Old Samuel was working in one of the flower beds and he straightened up as they passed and stared curiously at them.

"Don't you think they might ask?" said Emma. "We are pretty wet."

"I know," said Kylie miserably, "but..."

"My dad will kill me if he finds out," said Jason suddenly and both girls looked at him. "He'd forbidden me to climb the cliff."

"Come on," said Emma, rapidly reaching a

decision. "I'll smuggle you in. There's a back staircase that goes up from the kitchen. You can get up to your bedroom and change your clothes without anyone knowing."

Luckily the kitchen was empty with no sign of Mrs Bates and after Kylie and Jason had changed, Emma took their wet clothes and hung them on the clothes airer in her own bedroom.

Later she went down to the hotel lounge where she found Jason and Kylie watching the television.

They both seemed very quiet and not a bit like they had been before. Jason especially seemed very subdued.

"Those were your friends, weren't they?" asked Kylie as Emma sat down beside her on the sofa. "The ones you told us about."

"Yes," Emma nodded. "That was William and Charlotte and the older one was their brother, Albert."

"Didn't you say there was another boy?" asked Jason. He was sitting on the floor in front of the television and hadn't looked round when Emma had come into the room.

Now, as he looked over his shoulder, his expression was curious.

"Yes," Emma nodded, "there's Edward as well," she said. "I don't know where he was."

They were all silent for a while, although Emma suspected no one was really watching the television.

Then slowly, Kylie said, "They seemed a bit..." she hesitated.

"A bit what?" said Emma sharply.

"I don't know..." Kylie trailed off helplessly.

"Weird," said Jason shortly.

"They are not weird," retorted Emma.

"No, of course not," said Kylie hastily, glaring at her brother. "But you must admit, Emma," she went on after a moment, "there was something about them that seemed rather strange."

Emma took a deep breath. "I think what you're forgetting," she said tightly, "is that if it wasn't for my friends, we would all be dead by now."

Jason and Kylie remained silent as, angrily,

Emma went on, "They saved our lives whether you want to admit it or not."

"Yes," agreed Kylie after a moment in a very small voice. "Yes, they did. Of course they did. Do you think, Emma, we should do anything about it?"

"What do you mean? Do anything about it?" Jason's head jerked up. "I told you, I don't want Dad finding out what happened."

"I know you don't," said Kylie quickly, "but I just wondered if we should say thank you or something."

"We might not see them again," muttered Jason.

"You know where they live, don't you, Emma?" said Kylie.

"Yes," Emma nodded, an image of the house, pink in the evening sunlight coming into her mind, "yes, I know where they live."

At that moment Mrs Elliott came into the lounge.

"Oh, there you are," she said as Jason and Kylie scrambled guiltily to their feet. "I wondered where you had got to. Have you had a nice time?"

She didn't seem to notice they were wearing different clothes.

"Yes," said Kylie quickly, too quickly Emma thought, "we've had a brilliant time, haven't we, Jas?"

"Yeah," Jason mumbled, "brilliant."

"Good," said their mother brightly. "Well, it's time to come and get showered and changed now."

Without a word they obediently followed their mother out of the lounge and, leaving Emma alone, went off to change their clothes yet again.

Chapter 6

Emma sat very still for a long time, just thinking.

Kylie had said there had been something strange about the Carstairs family, Jason had called them weird, and now the more Emma thought about it, the more even she was forced to admit there had been something odd about them that day. Something odd about their behaviour and even about the way they had looked.

She wasn't exactly sure what it was and she had no idea what might have caused it, especially since only the night before William had seemed so happy when she had spoken to him in the garden of the big house.

Maybe she should simply go back to the house and ask them what had been wrong.

Yes, she thought, that was what she would do. She would go to the house and find them and she would do it right away.

But even as she came to her decision, a sudden noise at the window made Emma look up. To her dismay she realized the noise she had heard was the sound of rain against the window panes.

She stood up and, walking to the window, saw that thick grey clouds covered the sky. Standing on tiptoe she could just see the sea. It too looked grey and angry with white flecks in the waves. She shuddered as she thought what it would be like at that moment around the base of the cliffs. It had been bad enough earlier when the sun had been shining and the sea reasonably calm.

Now, the waves would be crashing over the rocks and the seagulls screaming above the wind.

And if it hadn't been for the Carstairs, for Albert, William and Charlotte, that was where she, and Jason, and Kylie would be now, under those waves at the base of the cliffs.

Kylie was right, the least they could do was to go and thank their rescuers. Tomorrow, Emma thought, when the weather improves, tomorrow she would take Kylie, Jason too if he wanted to go, to Darbhanga, to the house on the cliffs, to say thank you, and at the same time to find out what had been wrong.

The following morning Emma woke very early but was relieved to see that the sun was shining. Turning her head she saw that her mother in the other bed was also awake and was staring at the ceiling. Emma wondered if she was thinking about Dad.

She was just thinking she might ask, when Mum turned her head and looked at her.

"Hello," she said, smiling. "You're awake early. Special plans for today?"

"Not really," Emma yawned and stretched, not wanting for one minute for her mother to know what those plans were. "Thought I'd see what Jason and Kylie are doing," she added casually.

"I'm glad you've made friends with them," said Mum, "they seem nice."

"They're all right." Emma shrugged.

"What about those other friends, the ones on the beach? Have you seen them again?" asked Mum after a moment.

Emma stiffened. "Yes," she said, still, she hoped, casually, "I saw them yesterday actually … but … but I expect they'll be going back to London soon," she added, saying the first thing that came into her head. She had no idea really when the Carstairs family intended returning to London, she only knew she didn't want to discuss them in case her mother asked too many questions.

"That's the problem with summer visitors," said Mum, getting out of bed. "Here today and gone tomorrow. The Elliotts will go next week as well. Still, never mind, no doubt there will be others along to take their place."

Luckily Emma managed to catch Kylie on her own just as she was coming down the main staircase to join her family in the dining-room.

"I've been thinking," Emma said, "about

what you said yesterday. And I think you were right. We should thank the Carstairs for what they did. I thought I would go to their house this morning, that is if they aren't on the beach, and I wondered if you would like to come with me. Jason as well if he wants to."

"Yes, all right." Kylie nodded but Emma thought she looked really pleased that she had asked her. "I don't know about Jason though," she went on after a moment, "I don't think he'll want to come. I think he just wants to forget what happened."

Emma thought Kylie was probably right so it came as quite a surprise when they met by the hydrangeas at the arranged time and she saw that Jason was there too.

"What did you tell your parents?" asked Emma curiously.

"Just that we're going to the beach." Kylie shrugged. "They didn't mind. Besides, Dad has some business to do in Sandcoombe."

"Business?" Emma frowned as they began to walk down the path to the beach. "I thought you were on holiday."

"Dad's like that," said Jason. "He's always

involved in something or other."

The beach was empty but Emma wasn't really surprised. Somehow she hadn't expected the Carstairs to be there.

"So how do you get to their house?" asked Jason, standing for a moment and staring along the beach, his eyes shaded from the sun by the peak of his baseball cap.

"There's another path at the far end of the beach," explained Emma. "It's almost hidden by the trees, but it's there."

"Why did they go back out in the boat again yesterday?" asked Jason after a moment.

"I've no idea," said Emma. She too had wondered, but she wasn't going to admit as much to Jason.

"That girl," said Kylie suddenly, "Charlotte, she looked ... she looked sad. No, more than that, she looked like ... you know, Jason," she turned to her brother, "like Melanie Jones when she had that accident."

"Yes," Jason nodded in agreement, "shocked. That was it, she looked like she was in shock."

"Their clothes were rather strange as well," said Kylie as they set off along the beach.

"I think that's some sort of uniform that William was wearing," said Emma, rushing to defend her friends. "Sea Scouts or something like that."

"No," said Jason quickly, "it wasn't Sea Scouts. I know a boy in Sea Scouts and their uniform is nothing like that – it's much darker blue."

"And Charlotte's dress," added Kylie quickly before Emma could speak again, "it was beautiful – like something you'd wear to a party, not the sort of thing to wear in a boat."

"Well, they'd had a party the night before..." Still Emma tried to defend her friends but she could see from their expressions that she failed to convince the Elliotts.

"Anyway," she went on after a moment. "They must be very well off. They probably wear best clothes all the time. You just wait until you see their house. It's just like something out of a film ... it has balconies and a veranda..."

By this time they had reached the end of the beach and Jason, who was slightly ahead, was peering under the trees. "Is it up there?" he asked, looking over his shoulder at the two girls.

"Yes," Emma nodded.

"But it's so dark," said Kylie and Emma recognized fear in her voice. "It's like a tunnel."

"But it's not very long," said Emma as they began to climb the pathway which somehow seemed far more overgrown than it had before. "It's very steep, but not very long. There's a gate at the top, a white gate with the name Darbhanga painted on it."

"What's it mean?" asked Jason.

"I don't know." Emma shook her head. "I think I'll ask William. Ah, here we are," she puffed slightly as at last they reached the top of the path, "we'll soon be out in the sunshine again now, here's the gate..."

"Oh!" She stopped and stared. All that was left of the white painted gate was one stump of rotting wood. "Oh!" she said again, "it's gone. The gate's gone. But it was here, right here." She looked around her in bewilderment.

"Perhaps it's being repaired, or painted or

something," said Kylie helpfully.

But Emma hardly heard her for she had walked on through the bushes, out into the sunlight.

She stopped. Then she stared and stared in utter disbelief, for not only had the gate gone, but the house, Darbhanga, was no longer there either.

There was a large clearing where it had stood, a space amongst the trees, overgrown with a tangle of rambling pink roses and brambles and choked with waist-high weeds.

There was an eerie silence about the place while overhead, even the seagulls that swooped and circled were strangely quiet.

"So where is it then?" asked Jason, hands on hips as he gazed around.

"It was there. Right there," muttered Emma."

"Maybe you've made a mistake." Kylie was frowning. "Perhaps it's further along the cliffs."

"Maybe she dreamt it!" Jason sniggered, then fell silent as his sister shot him a furious look.

"I didn't dream it," retorted Emma. "It was here. I know it was." She began to walk towards the clearing and after only a moment's hesitation Kylie followed her.

"Well, there certainly was a house here once," said Jason as he too eventually joined the girls and they all reached the clearing. "Look, you can see the remains of the floor and the outline of the foundations. But it must have been years ago."

"It wasn't years ago," said Emma desperately, "it was the night before last. I saw it. It was here. There were lights on in the house – there was a party going on … people on the veranda. I saw Charlotte and her mother, I spoke to William on the lawn. He walked back to the gate with me."

"The gate that isn't there…?" Jason grinned.

"Jason, will you shut up," snapped Kylie. "This is upsetting enough for Emma as it is without you keeping on."

"All right." Jason shrugged, looking around him at the weeds, and the pieces of brick and plaster in the long grass. "If Emma saw all that only two nights ago, where is it now? It can't have disappeared that quickly."

"I don't know," said Kylie helplessly, "perhaps none of it was real..."

"Are you saying it was a dream as well?" demanded Emma, then not waiting for Kylie to reply, she swept on, "because if it was, how do you explain the rescue yesterday? You were there. Was that a dream too? And if it was, were we all in the same dream?" She stared in desperation from one to the other of them and saw that now even Jason looked disturbed.

"I don't know," he muttered, kicking at a chunk of plaster with the toe of his trainers. Then looking up quickly, he said, "I still think you've made a mistake, that this must be the remains of another house and that the one you saw is somewhere else."

"But where?" demanded Emma. "There was only the one pathway. It can't be anywhere else."

"Let's look," said Kylie. She was beginning to sound rather scared.

"All right," said Emma. "We'll look. But we

won't find it, because I tell you, it was right here. I know it was."

They searched for half an hour almost in silence, instinctively keeping close together. They looked behind the clearing, beyond the trees, but all that was there were fields and open countryside while on either side, along the cliffs in both directions spread dense bushes of yellow flowering gorse and broom.

In the end they were forced to admit defeat and it was a very subdued little group who finally stood beside the rotting gatepost and gazed back at the clearing.

Just for one moment Emma closed her eyes, and beyond the sound of the sea she fancied she could hear the music that had drifted across the cliffs that night from the party at Darbhanga.

"I know it was here," she whispered.

"Come on, Emma." Kylie touched her arm. "I think we should go."

"Yes, all right," Emma reluctantly agreed.

In almost total silence they made their way back through the dark tunnel of trees to the beach.

The sea was calm, the only evidence of the bad weather of the previous night a few pieces of driftwood that had been washed up on to the dry sand.

Emma stopped and gazed out to sea. At that moment she felt she would have given anything in the world just to see the green painted boat slip into view from around the headland.

But the bay was empty with hardly a ripple on the surface of the water and quite suddenly Emma was seized by an overwhelming fear that she might never see her friends again.

"What are you going to do now?" asked Jason suddenly, curiously.

"What do you mean?" Emma threw him a quick glance and saw that for once even he looked concerned.

"About your friends?" he added.

Emma looked out to sea again, then rapidly coming to a decision she straightened her shoulders, and said, "I'm afraid they might be in some sort of trouble, so I'm going to find them."

"We'll help," said Kylie enthusiastically. "Won't we, Jas?"

Her brother took a little longer to reply but at last even he nodded. "Yeah," he said, "I suppose it's the least we can do – after what they did for us."

Chapter 7

Emma didn't know where she should start searching for her friends any more than she knew what had happened to the house Darbhanga.

She had come to thc conclusion that the only possible explanation about the house was that she must have mistaken its location, because she was convinced she had seen it.

And if she'd seen it, there must be others who had seen it.

But who would know, not only about the house, but about the family who owned it? Who could she ask?

It should, she thought, be someone who knew about local people and their whereabouts, someone who had always lived in the area.

She found old Samuel in the garden dead-heading the rose bushes. It was very quiet, for the hotel guests were all at dinner, and the soft grass muffled even the sound of her approach.

Emma didn't think Samuel knew she was there, but as she stopped on the edge of the flower bed, without as much as even a glance in her direction, he said,

"Evenin' Miss Emma," then, pushing his battered hat to the back of his head, he added, "it's been a pretty day and no mistake – after that drop of rain last night."

"Er … yes, yes it has." Emma watched as Samuel took a pipe and a small leather pouch from the breast pocket of his blue overalls.

"Samuel –" she took a deep breath as carefully he took strands of tobacco from the pouch and stuffed them into the bowl of his pipe – "do you know a family by the name of Carstairs?"

"Eh?" Samuel looked up.

"The Carstairs family," repeated Emma

patiently. For some reason her heart had begun beating very fast and she found herself holding her breath as she waited for his reply.

"Well, now," Samuel said at last, maddeningly slowly, "wherever did you hear about them?"

"Oh, just around," said Emma quickly.

Samuel, searching in his pockets again, produced a box of matches with a triumphant flourish. "They used to be very well known in these parts," he said. "They were a well-to-do family..." He paused again, took out a match and struck it while Emma watched in an agony of suspense.

Cupping his hands around the bowl of the pipe Samuel lit the tobacco, puffing noisily. "He was something big in India," he continued at last. "Mr Carstairs that is – some diplomat or something."

"But where did they live?" asked Emma excitedly.

"Well, now," Samuel hesitated, pushing the spent match into his top pocket, "they had a big house in London..."

"But you said they were well known in

these parts," Emma interrupted.

"I was comin' to that," said Samuel. "They had a house here too, that were a big house an' all."

Suddenly Emma could contain herself no longer. "Was it called Darbhanga?" she cried. "The house, was that its name – Darbhanga?"

Samuel took the pipe from his mouth and stared at her in astonishment. "Whoever told you that?" he said, then, not waiting for a reply, he went on, "Yes that was it, Darbhanga – named after some place in India – or so my old mum used to say. The family used to come here every year for the summer..."

Emma stared at him. She hadn't been dreaming. She really had seen the house. "Do you know anything about the Carstairs children, Samuel?" she rushed on, suddenly afraid he was about to return to his roses.

"Eh? Children?" Samuel screwed up his face. "Well now, many years ago before she married my dad, my mum used to be nurse-maid for the Carstairs family. She used to tell us some stories, I can tell you..."

"But what about today," said Emma, "what about the Carstairs children now?"

Samuel frowned. 'I don't know," he said. "Haven't heard nothing about any of them for years now … except…" he paused.

"Yes?" said Emma eagerly. "Except for what?"

"Except for old Miss Carstairs of course."

"Miss Carstairs?"

Samuel nodded. "She's still alive, or at least she was last thing I heard. She lives at The Grange – must be well into her nineties now, I should think… Anyway, this won't do. I must get on with these roses." He turned away.

Emma watched him for a moment before she too turned to go back to the hotel, then on a sudden impulse, she stopped. "Samuel," she said again.

"Yes, Miss Emma?" he said.

"Where exactly is the house?"

"What house?" he said.

"Darbhanga."

"Oh, that. Well, it was further along the cliffs." Vaguely he pointed in the general direction. "Over there."

"What do you mean it was?" Once again Emma found she was holding her breath.

"It's not there now." Shaking his head Samuel leaned over a rose bush and began snipping again.

Emma's heart lurched. "Why isn't it there now?" she asked breathlessly.

"Because it was pulled down, demolished, years ago when I was a boy," said Samuel. "It were almost derelict and us kids used to play in it, but it weren't safe, so it had to be pulled down. Now, Miss Emma, I must get on with my work, otherwise I shall have your Grandma after me."

"So tell me again, what exactly did he say?" Kylie stared at Emma. It was later in the evening and after she had told them she needed to speak to them urgently, Kylie and Jason had joined Emma in the garden.

"He said he knew the Carstairs family or at least knew of them," said Emma patiently. "He also said that his mother used to work for them, and that there was a house called

Darbhanga and it was further along on the cliffs..."

"But that it isn't there now..." Jason finished the sentence for her. "I bet that was what he said."

Emma nodded. "Yes," she admitted with a sigh, "it was, and that's still the part that doesn't make any sense... But at least he knew what I was talking about..."

"So what did he say about the children?" asked Kylie excitedly. "Did he know them?"

"Well, he'd heard of children," Emma frowned, "but I don't think he meant William and Charlotte and the others because the children he'd heard of were ones who used to come here years ago. It's really confusing."

"Doesn't he know anything about the Carstairs family today?" asked Jason.

"No," Emma shook her head. "I don't think so. Although he did mention someone ... a Miss Carstairs who lives at a place called The Grange."

"Perhaps we could go and see her," said Kylie. "Maybe she's their auntie or something."

"What would we say?" asked Jason. "I

don't want anyone finding out about me climbing the cliffs."

"Honestly, Jason," snapped Kylie, "you're so selfish. Sometimes I think all you think about is yourself. I think we could go and see this Miss Carstairs and say that we are trying to get in touch with William and the others because we want to thank them for saving our lives. What do you think, Emma?"

"Well, yes," Emma agreed, "that's a very good idea, but the only thing is we don't know where The Grange is."

"I do," said Jason unexpectedly and as the girls looked at him in amazement, he went on, "I saw it the other day when we were going into Sandcoombe. It isn't far from here. We could easily walk there."

"We'll go tomorrow," said Emma.

"Dad said we are going out in the boat tomorrow." Jason looked at Kylie.

"I'll tell him we want to go out with Emma," replied Kylie firmly.

"OK," Jason nodded, "just as long as we don't have to take Charlene with us."

* * *

They didn't have to take Charlene with them the next morning because she went with her parents. As the Range Rover disappeared down the drive watched by Emma, Kylie and Jason, Emma turned and looked at the others.

"I'll have to tell my mum where we are going," she said. "You two come with me, she won't ask so many questions then."

They found Emma's mother in the kitchen with Mrs Bates. Both women looked up as they came in.

"Hello," Mum smiled at Kylie and Jason. "Off to the beach this morning?"

"No." It was Emma who replied. "At least, we might later, but first we are going to visit an old lady."

"An old lady?" Mum frowned.

"Yes," replied Emma, trying hard not to sound nervous. "She lives near here in a place called The Grange."

"The Grange?" Mrs Bates looked up. "She must have a bob or two if she lives there – dead posh that place."

"So who is she, Emma?" asked Mum curiously. "Is it someone you know?" She glanced quickly at Kylie then at Jason.

"Not exactly..." Kylie looked uncomfortable.

"It's someone Samuel Moses knows," said Emma suddenly. She wasn't sure that this was actually the case, but it sounded good. "Her name is Miss Carstairs and she's over ninety years old."

"Carstairs...? Carstairs...?" mused Mrs Bates, then looking at Emma she said, "isn't that the name of those friends of yours? The ones who were using the beach?"

"Yes, yes it is," said Emma, then hastily added, "Old Samuel told us that his mother worked for the Carstairs family many years ago... We just thought ... we thought..."

"That we would visit Miss Carstairs for Samuel..." continued Kylie.

"Yes," added Emma, "and tell her that I have met her relatives on the beach."

"Well, I think that's a lovely idea," said Mrs Bates. "You don't get many children who can be bothered to visit old folk today..." She trailed off, bending down and lifting some large baking trays from a cupboard. When she straightened up she turned and looked at Emma again. "Old Samuel's mother did you say?"

"Yes," Emma nodded, "she worked..."

"I remember her," said Mrs Bates. "She was still alive when I first came here to work for your gran. Maud her name was. I always thought it sounded strange ... Maud Moses. She lived with old Samuel until she died. She were well into her nineties too, you know."

"We'll be off now then, Mum," said Emma anxiously, sensing that Jason at least was growing bored with all this talk of the past.

To her relief her mother nodded. Just for one moment Emma had been afraid she had been going to say she didn't think they should go to The Grange.

But she didn't. Instead, she said, "Don't make a nuisance of yourselves, will you?"

"We won't," said Emma.

They almost fell out of the kitchen in their haste to get away and moments later they were running down the drive to the main Sandcoombe road.

Chapter 8

The Grange turned out to be a huge grey stone mansion set in acres of parkland and lovingly tended gardens.

"Surely she doesn't live here on her own?" said Kylie, gazing up the wide sweeping drive to the house. "It's much too big for one old lady."

"Perhaps we'll find that William and Charlotte and the others live here," said Jason.

"How can they?" demanded Emma. "They live at Darbhanga – some of the time at least – they told me so and I—"

"Yeah, I know," Jason cut her short, "you saw them there. But you can't get away from the fact that the house isn't there any more, can you?"

"Shut up, Jason," said Kylie. "We said we wouldn't mention that again until we find out what happened. Don't take any notice of him, Emma."

Emma fell silent and together the three of them began walking up the drive, their trainers crunching noisily on the loose gravel.

What Jason said had upset Emma a bit, but as they drew closer to the house she found herself wondering if he was right and if William and Charlotte and the others really did live here.

Maybe even now they were watching them from one of those windows.

She glanced up, but there was no movement inside the house.

What if they were there and turned out to be angry with them for coming here? It didn't bear thinking about somehow, and nervously Emma rubbed her damp hands down the side of her jeans.

On the other hand, they might be overjoyed to see them again. She brightened at that thought.

Why, she might only be moments away from seeing her friends again.

"You ring the bell, Emma," said Kylie as they came to a halt before the impressive front entrance of The Grange. The bell in question was a large brass affair that hung beside the studded wooden door.

"Shall I?" Emma hesitated.

"Oh, come on, I'll do it." Before either of the girls could do anything Jason had stepped forward and pulled the brass chain.

The bell clanged noisily and Emma gasped as the door was opened almost immediately, as if someone had indeed been watching them approach.

Emma wasn't sure who she had been expecting to answer the door, whether the old lady herself, or even one of her Carstairs friends, but it certainly wasn't the youngish, bright-faced lady in the nurse's uniform who stood facing them.

"Hello?" She smiled from one to the other of them. "What can I do for you?"

In spite of his earlier bravado Jason seemed struck dumb, likewise Kylie, so it was left to

Emma to do the talking.

"Oh," she said, "Oh, we're sorry to bother you, but we have come to see Miss Carstairs."

"Miss Carstairs? Well you'd better come in." The nurse stepped aside so that they could go into the house.

Just for the moment Emma seemed unable to move, as if her trainers had somehow become stuck in the gravel.

"Go on." She felt Kylie's hand pushing her slightly.

"Oh, right, yes," she said and walked up the three steps to the door then into the hall.

"Let's just make sure she's in her room," said the nurse, moving behind a desk and picking up a telephone. "She likes to walk in the grounds sometimes with some of the other residents. She really is remarkable for her age. Now, if she's there, who shall I say has come to see her?" She looked up and smiled again.

"Um ... say we are friends of Samuel Moses," said Emma, thinking rapidly. She knew it was no good simply saying their names because Miss Carstairs wouldn't have heard of them, unless of course Charlotte or William had told her about them. "Samuel's mother Maud used to work for the Carstairs family," she added as the nurse punched out a number on the telephone.

They watched in an agony of suspense as the nurse waited, then began to speak.

"Hello, Miss Carstairs?" she said. "Julia here. You have some young visitors. Yes." She paused then looked at Emma. "What's your name?" she said.

"Emma Thornton," Emma replied, then quickly added, "but she won't know me..."

"It's Emma Thornton." The nurse was speaking into the receiver again. "No, she said that," she went on, "she also said to tell you she is a friend of Samuel Moses ... yes, that's right, Moses. Apparently you may have known his mother ... Maud, was it?" she glanced at Emma who nodded eagerly.

"Yes, that's right, Maud," the nurse went on, then she paused again before saying. "All right, Miss Carstairs, yes of course."

"She says she would like to see you." The nurse replaced the receiver and smiled at the three of them. "Come on, I'll take you up to her suite."

She led the way up a wide, thickly-carpeted staircase then along a corridor with lots of dark wood panelling.

"You won't be able to stay for too long," she said, stopping before a closed door and lifting her hand to knock. "Miss Carstairs gets tired very quickly these days."

At first, when they entered, there didn't appear to be anyone in the room, then a voice came from the depths of a winged armchair that was turned towards the high arched windows.

"Come over here where I can see you."

Obediently they crossed the room and stood beside the chair, and Emma found herself gazing curiously down at its occupant.

Miss Carstairs was sitting very upright in the chair and the stare she turned upon them was both haughty and enquiring. She was wearing a lavender-coloured dress and a necklace of red stones. Her skin, crisscrossed with hundreds of tiny lines, reminded Emma of fine tissue paper.

"Do I know you?" she demanded, peering at each of them in turn.

"Not really, Miss Carstairs…" Emma began.

"So, what are your names?" demanded the old lady as the nurse went out of the room, leaving the door ajar.

"I'm Emma Thornton," said Emma, then quickly, before Miss Carstairs could interrupt again, she went on, "and these are my friends, Kylie Elliott and her brother Jason."

"Elliott?" said Miss Carstairs, glaring at Kylie. "Anything to do with the Oxfordshire Elliotts?"

"Er, no, I don't think so," said Kylie.

"Julia said something about Samuel Moses and Maud." Miss Carstairs looked at Emma again.

Emma took a deep breath. "Yes," she said, "that's right. Samuel Moses works for my grandmother, Mrs Cunningham, at the Seahorse Bay Hotel. He told me that many years ago his mother Maud worked for your family, Miss Carstairs—"

"Of course she did," Miss Carstairs interrupted. "Nanny Maud was our nursemaid."

"Yes," breathed Emma then hurried on, "Can you tell us something about your family, Miss Carstairs? You see, we met some of them recently and—"

"What do you want to know?" The old lady cut her short and Emma, glanced hastily at Kylie and Jason.

"Well, anything really..." she went on as Kylie nodded encouragingly at her.

"There were seven of us," said Miss Carstairs abruptly. "Not by any means a large family as families went. Large by today's standards of course. They haven't heard of large families these days. I had two sisters and four brothers. All dead now. I'm the only one left. One of my brothers was killed in action in France in the First World War. My youngest brother died last year."

"Oh, I'm sorry," said Emma. She didn't know what else to say.

"We really wanted to ask you about your family now," said Kylie suddenly.

"What?" The old lady frowned. "I just told you, I don't have any family now. I'm the only one left."

"Oh, we didn't mean your brothers and sisters," said Emma hastily, "we meant maybe … nephews or nieces … or," she hesitated, "maybe it would be great-nephews and nieces?"

"There aren't too many of those either," said Miss Carstairs. "Only two in fact and they live in New Zealand. They are my eldest sister's great-grandchildren. Look, over there –" she pointed to a bookcase in the far corner of the room – "get the family album and you can see for yourselves."

Slowly Emma got up and, watched by Kylie, Jason and Miss Carstairs, she crossed the room and, turning a tiny brass key, opened the glass doors of the bookcase.

"That's it, there," said Miss Carstairs, "the brown, leather book on the middle shelf."

Carefully Emma lifted the book down from the shelf and carried it to Miss Carstairs who took it from her and rested it across her knees.

They grouped around her, Emma kneeling beside the chair on one side, Kylie on the other, and Jason standing behind, while Miss

Carstairs opened the album and began turning the pages.

The first photograph looked very old. It was brownish in colour, its surface cracked and one corner creased as if it had been folded over at some time. It showed a man with a dark moustache and a lady in a long dress.

"Those are my parents," said Miss Carstairs. "We didn't have these new-fangled coloured photographs in those days, just sepia-tinted ones."

"He looks very strict," said Jason.

"He was," said Miss Carstairs. "But he was fair. Always fair. He was a diplomat in the Foreign Office for the Government, you know."

She turned the page and Emma found herself staring down at a photograph of Darbhanga.

Her breath caught in her throat.

"That's it!" she breathed. "That's Darbhanga!" It was just as she had seen it. Just as she remembered; the balconies, the veranda, the long lace curtains at the windows.

"You've heard of Darbhanga?" Miss

Carstairs sounded surprised while Kylie and Jason leaned forward for a better look.

"Oh, yes," whispered Emma. "I..." She was about to say she'd seen it, had been there, but Miss Carstairs interrupted again.

"It was the most beautiful house," she said, "and in such a glorious position overlooking the Channel, although..." she paused, "after the tragedy my mother never liked it. Never wanted to go there. It was different for me, I suppose, I was too young at the time to understand what had happened, and of course, I hardly knew him."

She turned the page again and a beautiful young woman stared up at them. A woman with thick dark hair piled high on to the top of her head.

"My oldest sister," murmured Miss Carstairs. "It's her great-grandchildren I was telling you about in New Zealand. Wait a minute, I have a picture of them ... I put it with their great-grandmother's photograph."

Emma leaned forward eagerly, holding her breath as Miss Carstairs fumbled in a little pocket on the back of the page.

Then two young woman were smiling back at her from a shiny, coloured photograph. Both were tall, very slim and had long blonde hair. From the likeness they were quite obviously sisters, but Emma's heart sank for she had never seen either of them in her life before.

"I have another photograph of Olivia, their great-grandmother," Miss Carstairs was saying, but Emma hardly heard her for she was too busy wondering where Charlotte and William and the others could be.

Just for the moment there when Miss Carstairs had said her only relatives were her sister's great-grandchildren, she had thought it must be them, that they had been here on holiday from their home in New Zealand.

"It's a group photograph." Miss Carstairs turned the page again and Emma forced herself to concentrate. "It's taken on the beach," she went on, "the beach below Darbhanga – quite near here, but Olivia is on it. That's her at the back."

The photograph was a little blurred but it did indeed show a group of people on the beach. Emma narrowed her eyes and leaned forward even further.

"Oh, look," said Kylie. "It is the beach – you can see the cliffs behind."

Emma frowned. Kylie was quite right, but there was something else about the photograph that was familiar, not just the beach and the cliffs. Something to do with the people themselves. And with the rug spread on the sand beneath a sunshade, the lady with a straw hat with a baby on her knee and the other figures, mostly children sitting on the sand or leaning against the side of a rowing boat.

"When was this photograph taken?" asked Emma.

"Dear me, I don't know, I'm sure," said Miss Carstairs blinking rapidly. "It was before the tragedy of course. And I was just a toddler – there I am with Nanny Maud – look, that's her," she pointed to the lady with the straw hat, "so well, now, let me see, I'm ninety-two – so this must have been taken about ninety years ago."

It was Jason who broke the silence that followed.

"What was the tragedy?" he asked. His voice sounded strange, not like Jason's voice at all.

"My brother," said Miss Carstairs. "He was only eleven. They were celebrating Olivia's engagement with a party at Darbhanga, or so I've been told. Some of them went moonlight swimming in the bay and he was drowned..." She paused and Emma felt the tiny hairs on the back of her neck begin to prickle.

"His body was never found, you know," Miss Carstairs went on, "even though my other brothers and my youngest sister searched and searched in our family boat – they never found his body."

She peered at the photograph again. "There he is," she pointed, "that's him there in his sailor suit – the boys always wore sailor suits in those days you know – but it's blurred, not very clear. Wait a minute, there is a better one of him here somewhere." She turned several pages.

"Here it is," she said at last. "This one was taken with my other sister, and the brother who lost his life in the Great War."

Emma gazed down at the photograph of the three children. Charlotte, her dark hair tumbling over her shoulders and her wicked eyes dancing with merriment, gazed back.

William's expression was also just as she remembered, serious yet concerned as he too seemed to look straight into her eyes.

Their brother was seated between them, as fair as they were dark, but his smile was somehow remote, his gaze far away.

"That's him." Miss Carstairs's finger trembled as she pointed. "That's Edward."

There was a long silence in the room, broken only by the ticking of a clock on the mantelpiece.

In the end it was Emma who spoke, finding her voice from somewhere, to ask just one question. "Miss Carstairs," she said, "can you tell me please, what is your Christian name?"

"My Christian name?" She sounded surprised. "Why, it's Louise," she said and as the old lady looked up, Emma thought she caught the gleam of tears in her eyes.

Chapter 9

"They were ghosts."

It was Kylie who said it as they walked away from The Grange, their feet crunching on the gravel; a white-faced, shaking Kylie.

"Don't be ridiculous," said Jason. "Of course they weren't ghosts."

"So what were they then?" Kylie threw Emma a fearful glance but Emma didn't speak. Her head felt as if it was about to burst and she needed time to sort out all they had heard.

"Well, they certainly weren't ghosts," said Jason, but even he sounded far from sure. "Ghosts," he went on with an uneasy glance over his shoulder, "are flimsy things, you can see right through them. They weren't ghosts.

That one that rescued me he was solid – his back was like … like…" he searched round for a suitable comparison, "like an ox!" he said at last. "He certainly wasn't a ghost."

"How do you know?" Emma spoke at last.

"What do you mean?" Jason frowned.

"How do you know what ghosts are like if you've never seen one?"

"Well, everyone knows … don't they?" Jason shrugged helplessly.

"If they weren't ghosts," asked Kylie slowly, "what do you think they were?"

"Who," said Emma sharply, "who do you think they were, not what." She hesitated, then she said, "I'm not sure, I only know they were real people. I saw them and so did you, so they must have been there."

"If they were ghosts," said Kylie slowly, "it means they came back. I saw this programme once on the telly where they said that ghosts are the spirits of dead people and that when they come back it's usually for a reason. Do you think the reason they came back was to search for Edward's body?"

"You heard what Miss Carstairs said," she

went on when Emma and Jason remained silent, "she said they searched for his body in their boat."

"But Emma had seen them before that," said Jason.

"I tried to warn them..." said Emma in a small voice. "I told William that it wasn't safe to swim in the bay. Oh, why didn't he listen to me! If only he had, Edward wouldn't have drowned."

No one spoke, then as they reached the end of the drive Jason suddenly said, "But if they hadn't been out searching in the boat, they wouldn't have found us... Then we would have drowned, wouldn't we?"

The girls stared at him.

"I think," he went on slowly after a moment, "that it wasn't that they came back at all, I think it was us."

"What do you mean, us?" asked Emma in bewilderment.

"Well," said Jason seriously, "if they had come back into our world they would have been ghosts, but we didn't think they were ghosts, did we?"

The girls shook their heads and eagerly, he went on, "So that means we must have slipped back in time into their world."

"You mean like in Doctor Who?" said Kylie excitedly.

"Something like that, yes." Jason nodded.

"But why?" demanded Emma. "Why should we have done that?"

"So that when we were in trouble, because they were in their boat searching for Edward, they were also there to rescue us," said Jason triumphantly.

"It's the only other explanation if we don't believe they were ghosts," he went on after a moment. "I don't think you could have prevented Edward being drowned, Emma, because it had already happened, but they could prevent us drowning, because it hadn't happened yet. And anyway," he paused, "there's another reason they couldn't have been ghosts."

"What's that?" Emma threw him a fearful glance, wondering what on earth he might be about to say next.

"We're all agreed, you have to be dead to be a ghost..."

"But they are," said Emma. "You heard Miss Carstairs, they are all dead – William, Charlotte, Olivia... Oh!" her hand flew to her mouth as it suddenly dawned on her what he meant. "You mean...?"

"Yep," Jason nodded and thrust his hands into the pockets of his jeans. "She's still alive, isn't she? Wasn't she one of them that you saw?"

Emma nodded slowly. "Yes," she said, "she was the little girl on the tartan rug. George was the baby, but Louise was the little girl... And the nursemaid I saw, the one I thought was an au pair girl, must have been old Samuel's mother, Maud... But ... you're quite right, Jason," she said excitedly, "Louise, that is, Miss Carstairs, certainly couldn't have been a ghost."

"So what's it all mean?" wailed Kylie. "I still don't understand."

"It's like I said," said Jason, hunching his shoulders, "we slipped back in time. Emma did it first when she met the Carstairs, then again when she saw the house. Then we did it as well when we were all rescued."

"That's why they looked so strange, so shocked," said Emma slowly. "Because Edward was missing."

"It's still dead spooky," said Kylie, then she went on, "Do you think it will happen again? Do you think we will ever see them again, Charlotte and William and Albert?"

"Shouldn't think so." Jason shrugged. "Not unless we need rescuing again. Even then, I shouldn't count on it – they might not be there another time."

They were silent after that, each trying to come to terms with all that had happened, then as the Seahorse Bay Hotel came into sight, Jason said, "I still don't think we should tell anyone..."

"You're still afraid of Dad finding out that you climbed the cliff," said Kylie."

"I know," admitted Jason, "but that's not the only reason."

"You don't think anyone would believe us, do you?" Emma threw him a quick glance.

"Well, what do you think?" said Jason.

Emma shook her head.

"OK," said Kylie, "so it stays a secret, our

secret for ever and ever. Agreed?"

"Agreed." They all nodded and in silence went into the hotel where they found Mr and Mrs Elliott in the hall with Charlene.

"Oh, there you are," said Mrs Elliott, "good. We have something to tell you. Come into the lounge. You too, Emma," she added when Emma would have hung back.

Emma's mother and her grandmother were already in the lounge and Emma wondered what was happening.

For one dreadful moment she thought perhaps they had found out. A quick look at Jason showed that he too feared the same.

"We've just been to the solicitor's office in Sandcoombe," said Mr Elliott when he had everyone's attention, "and we thought you might like to know that we have definitely decided we shall be coming here to live."

Emma looked up quickly. Only a short while ago she would have hated the idea of living near the Elliott family, but that was all different now, and she found herself listening eagerly to their father.

"As you know," he said, "I'm a builder."

Emma hadn't known, but as her grandmother and mother were nodding she assumed they must have known.

"I've always wanted to build my own house," Mr Elliott continued, "but I've never been able to find the right spot. Well," he smiled, "all that's changed now. We've found the perfect place. Haven't we, love?"

He glanced at his wife, who smiled and nodded.

"It's a plot of land on the cliffs very near here," he went on, "and it's been for sale for some time. Apparently, there was a house there many years ago, a house called Darbhanga."

Emma gasped and she and Jason and Kylie exchanged startled glances. Mr Elliott didn't seem to notice for he carried on talking.

"There's a clause in the deeds that says that any other dwelling that is built there, should be called by the same name. So," he glanced round at them all, "that's what we're going to do. We shall build a house, we shall call it Darbhanga and very soon, we will be your new neighbours."

* * *

"Are you pleased?" asked Mum later.

"Yes," Emma nodded. "Yes I am, very pleased."

"I was afraid you wouldn't be," said Mum. "You didn't seem to like them at first."

"I didn't really know them then," replied Emma. "I do now and we've become friends. I can't wait for them to come here to live."

"I'm so pleased," said Mum. She paused. "Are you going to get ready for bed now?"

"No," Emma shook her head. "Not just now. I'm going to go down to the beach, just for a little while. I won't be long."

"All right." Mum nodded.

It was almost as if she understood. But that was impossible. How could anyone understand what had happened?

Quietly Emma slipped away from the hotel. Much as she enjoyed the company of the others, she needed, at that moment, to be on her own.

The tide was out and the sun was just slipping behind the horizon. Emma sat down, buried her toes in the dry sand and, hugging her knees, gazed out to sea.

What she had told her mother had been true. She was pleased the Elliott family were coming to Seahorse Bay to live.

"But do you mind about Darbhanga?" Kylie had asked her anxiously after the adults had gone.

"Why should I mind?" she'd replied.

"I don't know really," Kylie had shrugged. "It's just that I suppose I think of Darbhanga as somehow being especially yours."

And it still will be, thought Emma.

Closing her eyes she lifted great handfuls of sand, letting it run through her clenched fists.

The new Darbhanga might belong to the Elliotts, and it really would be nice having them nearby and always able to share their secret, but the old Darbhanga belonged to the Carstairs family, to William, to Charlotte, to Edward and the others, and to her, Emma, because she was the only one who had actually seen it.

She still wasn't completely sure what had happened. Whether they had been ghosts who had returned to her world, or whether Jason's idea was right and she and the Elliotts had slipped back to another time. Somehow it didn't matter, because whatever it had been, it had happened, and the memory was there for ever.

Still sifting the sand, Emma rested her head on her knees and after a while she fancied she heard voices.

And quite suddenly they were there again. She could hear them, calling and laughing to each other; and she could see them, running across the wet sand.

Charlotte, her black hair streaming behind her, her frilled skirts tucked up above her knees, William and Edward, paddling in the shallow water helping Albert with the green painted boat, and Nanny Maud, sitting with Louise and the baby George on the tartan rug beneath the white sunshade.

It was just as it had been before, but as the sun finally sank beneath the horizon, Emma lifted her head and blinked, for once again the beach was deserted, the waves were breaking gently on the shimmering wet sand and the only sound was the cry of the seagulls as they circled overhead.

Then, as she would have let the last handful of sand trickle away, Emma felt something sharp dig into her skin.

Opening her fingers she looked down, and there in the palm of her hand, rusted from the salty air, discoloured by the sand, lay a girl's hairslide – a pretty hairslide in the shape of a butterfly.